For Sean Sekora, with love.

COUNTING SHEEP

by George Mendoza
Illustrated by Kathleen Reidy

Publishers • GROSSET & DUNLAP • New York

Library of Congress Catalog Card Number: 81-84016. ISBN: 0-448-12041-0. Text Copyright © 1982 by Ruth Sekora.
Illustrations Copyright © 1982 by Kathleen Reidy.

There was an old shepherd who counted
sheep each night to fall asleep. . . . One, two,
three, four, he would count as the little sheep
jumped over the fence.

But one night, when the old shepherd was
under the stars, under his favorite tree, high
up on a hill with his eyes closed tight, he had a
troubled dream that made him toss and turn
and roll. And this is what he dreamt:

ONE sheep was off conducting a wild
chorus of night-croaking frogs.
    The old shepherd rolled one restless turn
down the hill.

TWO sheep were at The Night Bird Cafe
being sketched by owls and hawks.
  The old shepherd rolled two restless turns
down the hill.

THREE sheep had jumped a freight train clanking through the dead of night. The old shepherd rolled three restless turns down the hill.

FOUR sheep were on a fox hunt with bugles blaring across the fields and woods. The old shepherd rolled four restless turns down the hill.

5

FIVE sheep were dancing at a lavish
costume ball.
The old shepherd rolled five restless turns
down the hill.

SIX sheep were racing down the track
in the Grand Prix.
   The old shepherd rolled six restless turns
down the hill.

SEVEN sheep had gone off to sea in a seven-masted schooner.
The old shepherd rolled seven restless turns down the hill.

EIGHT sheep were playing hide-and-go-seek.
The old shepherd rolled eight restless turns
down the hill.

NINE sheep were climbing the world's highest mountain.
The old shepherd rolled nine restless turns down the hill.

TEN sheep were skydiving.
The old shepherd had rolled halfway down
the hill.

ELEVEN sheep had formed their own band.
The old shepherd rolled eleven restless turns
down the hill.

TWELVE sheep were dueling in a
fencing tournament.
The old shepherd rolled twelve restless
turns down the hill.

THIRTEEN sheep were running in a marathon.

The old shepherd rolled thirteen restless turns down the hill.

FOURTEEN sheep were skating across the ice.
The old shepherd rolled fourteen restless turns down the hill.

FIFTEEN sheep were playing cowboys
and Indians.
  The old shepherd rolled fifteen restless turns
down the hill.

SIXTEEN sheep were attending Sunday school.

The old shepherd rolled not one restless turn down the hill.

SEVENTEEN sheep were all stacked up
in a wobbly pyramid.
  The old shepherd rolled seventeen restless
turns down the hill.

EIGHTEEN sheep were at the seaside
dashing in and out of the waves.
The old shepherd rolled eighteen restless
turns down the hill.

NINETEEN sheep were kicking up
their heels in a Parisian chorus line.
The old shepherd rolled nineteen restless
turns down the hill.

TWENTY sheep were carrying the old shepherd, who had fallen asleep at the bottom of the hill, back up to his favorite tree on top of the hill.

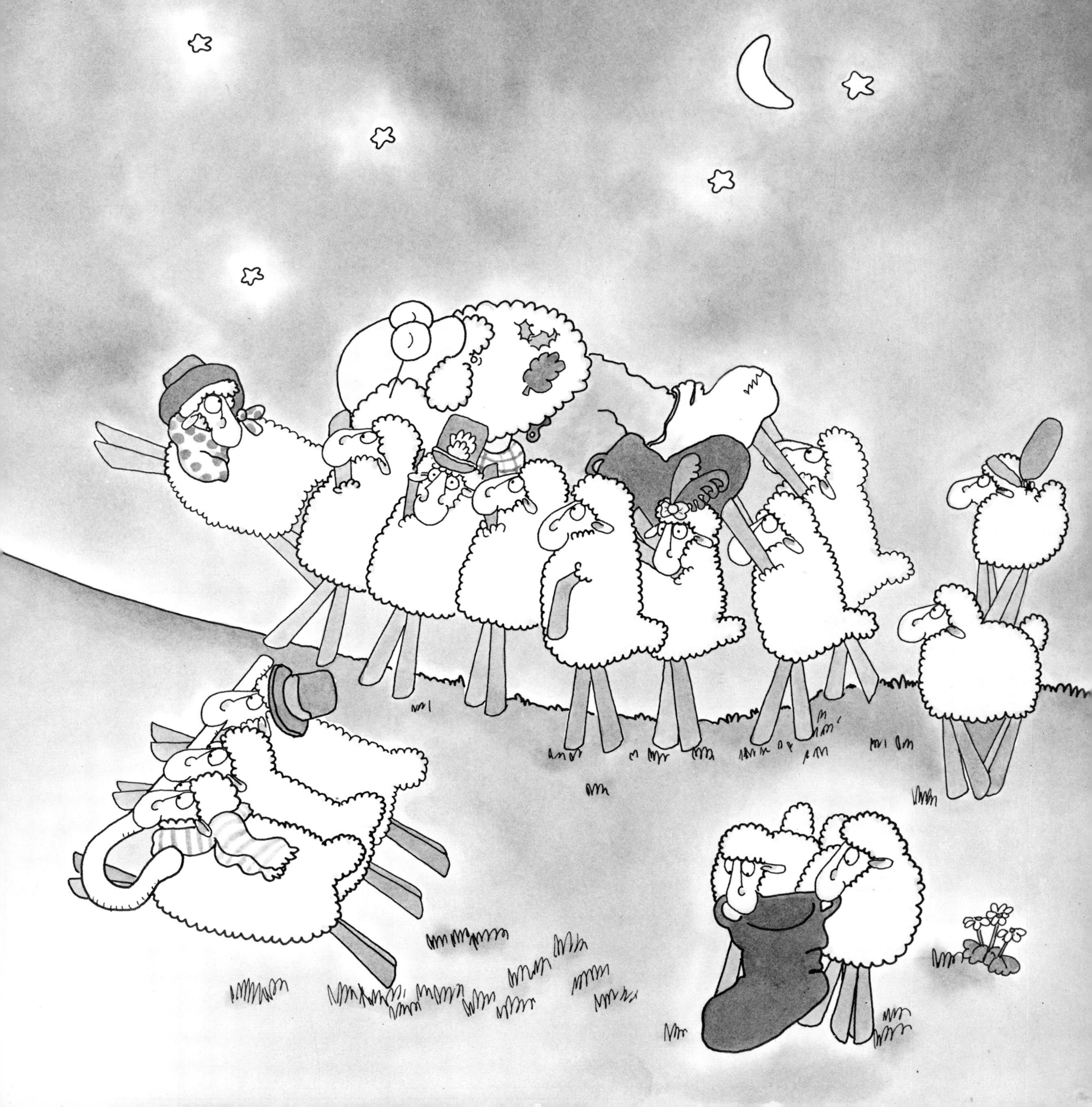